Emily's Death

Emily's Death

Dawn Naugle

Copyright © 2023 by Dawn Naugle.

Library of Congress Control Number:		2023914864
ISBN:	Hardcover	979-8-3694-0502-4
	Softcover	979-8-3694-0501-7
	eBook	979-8-3694-0500-0

All rights reserved. No part of this book may be reproduced or transmitted in any form or by any means, electronic or mechanical, including photocopying, recording, or by any information storage and retrieval system, without permission in writing from the copyright owner.

This is a work of fiction. Names, characters, places and incidents either are the product of the author's imagination or are used fictitiously, and any resemblance to any actual persons, living or dead, events, or locales is entirely coincidental.

Any people depicted in stock imagery provided by Getty Images are models, and such images are being used for illustrative purposes only.
Certain stock imagery © Getty Images.

Print information available on the last page.

Rev. date: 08/08/2023

To order additional copies of this book, contact:
Xlibris
844-714-8691
www.Xlibris.com
Orders@Xlibris.com
787088

Contents

Chapter 1   The Return of Emily.......................... 1

Chapter 2   Emily's Revolution 5

Chapter 3   A Faithful Plunge............................ 13

Chapter 4   The Pool Accident..........................17

Chapter 5   The Message from Beyond............. 23

Chapter 6   Emily's Journey to the Light of
             Heaven 33

Chapter One

The Return of Emily

Once upon a time in the small, picturesque town of Willowdale, a young girl named Emily decided to move back to her old hometown after many years. She yearned for the familiar streets, the comforting faces, and the nostalgic memories that had shaped her childhood. Little did she know that her return would unravel a chilling mystery that had long been buried in the depths of time. As Emily settled into her childhood home, strange occurrences began to unfold. At first, it was subtle—a flickering light here, a creaking floorboard there. But as days turned into weeks, the strange happenings grew more frequent and unsettling. Objects would move on

their own, whispers would float through the air, and eerie shadows danced along the walls. Her friends, Shara and Mark started to act every strangely as if they were ignoring her. They would leave her cats out and when she would tell them I told you I don't let my cats out it was if she was never heard which left her very angry, confused and frightened.

Chapter Two

Emily's Revolution

Emily had always felt like an outsider. Ever since she was a child, she had this overwhelming sense of being watched, of being haunted. Strange occurrences surrounded her wherever she went. Shadows danced at the corners of her vision, objects moved without explanation, and whispers echoed in her ears when no one else was around. Emily couldn't shake the feeling that she was being haunted by ghosts. But little did she know that the truth was far stranger than she could have ever imagined. As the days went by the inexplicable events intensified. Desperate for answers, Emily delved into paranormal research, reading countless books and visiting

haunted locations, hoping to find a connection to the spirit world. She was convinced that she was being haunted by restless souls, desperately trying to communicate with her. One fateful night, Emily found herself back in her old home town house. on the outskirts of town. Armed with her camera and a voice recorder, Emily stepped into the darkness, her heart pounding with anticipation and fear. As she explored the dilapidated rooms, she couldn't help but notice how the air felt heavy, almost suffocating. The floorboards creaked under her weight, and a chill ran down her spine. But instead of being afraid, Emily was filled with a strange sense of familiarity. as if this house held some deep, hidden secret about her own existence. Venturing into the attic, Emily stumbled upon an old journal, its pages yellowed with age. Intrigued, she dusted it off and began to read. The words on the page seemed to leap out at her, revealing the truth she had been seeking for so long. The journal belonged to her friend Sarah, who is living in the now. But how could that be Emily thought to herself, this is my house. The entries chronicled her growing suspicion that

she was being haunted by a ghost, a presence that seemed to mimic her every move. But as Emily read on, she realized the horrifying truth: she had come to the realization that she herself was the ghost all along and her friend Sarah is Indeed the occupant of this house. The pieces of the puzzle fell into place for Emily. Everything suddenly made sense—the strange occurrences, the feeling of being watched, the whispers that only she could hear. Her friend leaving her cats out and then not listening to her. She indeed was the ghost haunting her own life. The living people she had seen, the ones she believed were the ghosts, were in fact the real living beings, going about their lives while she unknowingly watched from the other side. Overwhelmed by this revelation, Emily sank to the floor, the weight of the truth pressing down on her. She had spent her entire so called life searching for answers, only to discover that the answers were within her all along. Tears streamed down her face as she mourned the loss of the life she thought she had. The life she could never truly be a part of. But as the initial shock subsided, a newfound sense of purpose emerged within Emily.

She may be a ghost, but she was determined to make her presence known. to connect with the living in a way she had never thought possible. She would no longer be a silent observer. She would become an active participant in the world she had once believed to be beyond her reach. Armed with this revelation, Emily left the house. her steps filled with newfound determination. She would embrace her spectral existence and find a way to bridge the gap between her and the reason she is a ghost.

Chapter Three

A Faithful Plunge

Emily sought solace in the local community library after reading the journal she had found. She delved into the town's history, searching for answers to the peculiar events that plagued Emily's life. There her investigation led her to the town's archives, where she uncovered a long-forgotten newspaper article dated several years ago. The article detailed a tragic incident involving a young woman named Emily, who had drowned in her backyard pool on a fateful summer's night. The chilling realization struck her leveling chills going down her back and goosebumps appearing all over her body suddenly feeling a slight coldness with in the room. The girl

who had returned to Willowdale was not alive. Emily was a ghost who had come home to her final resting place unknowingly. But why? Was there more to the accident or was there something she needed to finish before she could move on, she thought to herself? As she thought that to herself, Emily's memories flashed before her eyes, and she struggled to grasp the truth. Fragments of that ill-fated night began to resurface. She remembered feeling tired and disoriented after a night of revelry. In her inebriated state, she had stumbled and fallen into the pool, her cries for help swallowed by the night.

Chapter Four

The Pool Accident

As Emily stood at the edge of the pool, her vision blurred by the hazy effects of alcohol. It had been a night of celebration, filled with laughter and carefree moments. But now, in her intoxicated state, the world seemed to spin around her. She had lost her balance several times already, yet stubbornly refused to acknowledge the danger. Her friends, Sarah and Mark, watched with growing concern. They had tried their best to discourage Emily from going near the pool, knowing the risks involved. But their pleas fell on deaf ears, drowned out by Emily's drunken determination to take a late-night dip. "Emily, please, you've had enough," Sarah said,

her voice tinged with worry. "Let's go inside and get some rest." But Emily dismissed her friend's concerns with a careless wave of her hand. "I'm fine, Sarah, don't worry about me. I just want to cool off a bit." I'm really hot. In her unsteady state, Emily took a few unsteady steps closer to the pool's edge. The flickering glow of the moon danced on the surface of the water, beckoning to her. Ignoring the wavering reflection, she tentatively dipped one foot into the pool. Sarah's and marks heart raced as they saw Emily teetering on the edge. "Emily, please be careful! You're not in any condition to swim", Sarah yelled out. Just then Mark, feeling a sense of urgency, quickly moved to intervene. "Emily, it's not worth the risk. Let's go inside and rest. We can swim another day." But before anyone could react, Emily lost her balance. Her body tipped forward, arms flailing in a futile attempt to regain stability. The world seemed to move in slow motion as she toppled over the edge, her body plunging into the water with a loud splash. Panic gripped Sarah and Mark as they rushed to the pool's edge. In a flurry of fear and adrenaline, they dove into the water,

desperately searching for their friend. Seconds felt like an eternity as they scanned the depths, their hands frantically reaching out, hoping to find a sign of Emily. Finally, Mark's hand brushed against something solid. With renewed determination, he pulled Emily's lifeless body to the surface. Gasping for air, he and Sarah carried her out of the water and onto the pool deck. Time seemed to stand still as they performed CPR, desperately trying to revive their dear friend. But despite their efforts, Emily remained unresponsive. The accident had taken its toll, and the consequences were irreversible. Mark called 911 and as sirens wailed in the distance, Sarah clutched Emily's hand, tears streaming down her face. Mark, his voice choked with emotion, whispered, "I'm so sorry, Emily. We should have done more to prevent this." We tried but it was too late. now your gone and it's all are faults.

Chapter Five

The Message from Beyond

With newfound understanding, Emily embarked on a mission to bring peace to her friend's emotional attachment to the accident and help them realize they indeed was not at fault and did all they could so Emily's restless spirit can rest at peace. After a while of trying to let Shara and Mark know that her spirit was with them They sought the guidance of an elderly town resident known for her clairvoyant abilities. The wise woman revealed that Emily's spirit had remained trapped in Willowdale, unable to move on due to her untimely demise. Her need to let them know they didn't have to feel sorry or at fault anymore. Together, they devised a plan to help

Emily find closure. They organized a gathering at Emily's childhood home, inviting friends and family who had known her in life.

As the night unfolded, bittersweet memories were shared, tears were shed, and forgiveness was granted. Amidst the gathering, a sense of tranquility descended upon the house. Emily's spirit appeared, her ethereal presence shimmering in the moonlight. With tears of both joy and sadness. The moon cast an ethereal glow over the darkened room as Emily's friends gathered for a unique experience. They had sought solace in the presence of a medium, hoping to find closure and absolution for a heavy burden they had carried for far too long. Guilt had consumed them, as if their every action had played a role in the tragic events that had unfolded. But little did they know that this night would bring them a profound revelation. one that would heal their wounded souls and grant them the peace they so desperately sought. The room was adorned with flickering candles. their gentle flames dancing in the stillness. An air of anticipation hung heavy, mingling with a mixture

of hope and trepidation. Emily's friends, Sarah and mark sat in a circle. their hands clasped tightly together. their hearts ready to receive any word from the other side. The medium, a serene woman named Madeline, sat at the center of the circle, her eyes closed in deep concentration. Her connection to the spiritual realm was well-known. her abilities acknowledged by those who sought her guidance. She had dedicated her life to helping others find solace through contact with departed loved ones. As the minutes ticked by, the room grew quieter, the silence broken only by the soft rustle of fabric and the gentle hum of anticipation. Suddenly, Madeline's eyes fluttered open, revealing irises that seemed to hold ancient wisdom. She took a deep breath and began to speak in a voice that seemed to resonate with an otherworldly power. "Emily, can you hear me? Your friends have gathered here tonight. They are bearing the weight of guilt and remorse. They blame themselves for what transpired, but you wish to tell them otherwise. You want them to know it wasn't their fault. that they should release the burden they have carried for far too long. Guilt has

consumed them for way to long. " The words hung in the air, carrying a profound sense of relief and understanding. Tears welled up in the eyes of Sarah and mark as they listened to the medium's message. It was as if Emily's voice echoed through the room. reaching deep into their souls, assuaging their guilt and offering forgiveness. Madeline continued, her voice gentle yet resolute. "Emily wants you to know that she holds no blame towards any of you. She understands the complexities of life and the unpredictable nature of events. She wants you to find peace within yourselves. to let go of the guilt that has shackled your hearts for far too long." Emotions surged through the room, a mix of sorrow, relief, and gratitude. Sarah and mark felt a weight lift from their shoulders, as if an invisible burden had been lifted. The darkness that had clouded their minds began to dissipate, replaced by a glimmer of hope and healing. Madeline concluded the message, her voice filled with compassion. "Emily sends her love to each one of you. She wants you to live your lives to the fullest. She wants you to honor her memory by embracing joy and finding happiness.

She will always be with you, a guiding light in your darkest hours." She'll always be looking after you and protecting you. She says she is at fault for her accident not no one else. As the words settled in their hearts, Emily's friends embraced each other, their tears mingling in a shared release of emotions. In that moment, they made a silent vow to honor Emily's memory and to live lives filled with purpose and love.

Chapter Six

Emily's Journey to the Light of Heaven

An overwhelming feeling of love and serenity filled the room. It was as if the very fabric of the universe had paused to acknowledge the passage of a beautiful soul. As Emily's spirit started to walk towards the light she was greeted by a celestial chorus of voices. harmonizing in a chorus of love and welcome. The light that had surrounded her grew brighter, enveloping her with a warmth and peace beyond human comprehension. She embarked on a journey into the realm of pure love, leaving behind the constraints of earthly existence. And so, she bid her loved ones' farewell, finally ready to embrace the afterlife. From that day onward, Willowdale regained

its peaceful aura, and the strange happenings ceased. The town had laid its restless spirit to rest and would forever remember the girl who had returned home, unknowingly completing her unfinished journey. the tale of Emily's haunting became a legendary story whispered by the townsfolk of Willowdale, a cautionary reminder of the importance of finding closure and making amends before departing from this world.

Notes

Notes

Notes

Notes

Notes

Notes